D1394976

Gumdrop

and Horace

Val Biro

CLAREMONT BOOKS

Published by the Penguin Group
Penguin Books Ltd, 27 Wrights Lane, London
W8 5TZ, England
Penguin Books Australia Ltd, Ringwood,
Victoria, Australia
Penguin Books Canada Ltd, 10 Alcorn Avenue,
Toronto, Ontario, Canada M4V 3B2
Penguin Books (NZ) Ltd, 182-190 Wairau Road,
Auckland 10, New Zealand

Penguin Books Ltd, Registered Offices:
Harmondsworth, Middlesex, England

This edition first published in Great Britain in 1982
by Hodder and Stoughton

This edition published by Claremont Books,
an imprint of Godfrey Cave Associates Limited,
42 Bloomsbury Street, London, WC1B 3QJ,
under licence from Val Biro, 1996

Copyright © 1982 Val Biro

ISBN 1 854 71788 X

'Come on, Horace,' said Mr Oldcastle to his little black dog, 'we are going to do some shopping in town.'

'Shopping' usually meant 'food' to Horace, and he liked the sound of that. So he leapt into the back of Gumdrop. Mr Oldcastle shut the door and they were off.

Horace enjoyed the fresh air as they drove along. He liked sniffing at the scenery as it flashed by. It was a sort of smellyvision to him. And it smelt even better when Gumdrop's hood was down.

When Gumdrop was safely parked near the shops, Mr Oldcastle got out.

'Now be a good boy and wait here until I come back,' he told Horace. 'Don't leave Gumdrop, whatever you may sniff around here.'

He patted Horace on the head and went into a big shop round the corner.

It was a little boring for Horace just to sit there all by himself. All he could do was to look at all the people and sniff at the delicious smells all around him. Those loaves were very appetising, but he remembered what Mr Oldcastle had said.

Then something else wafted into his nose. The most delicious smell he could have wished for. His very favourite flavour of all: SAUSAGES! This was too much for the dog. He forgot what Mr Oldcastle had said and jumped out of Gumdrop to investigate.

There they were! Three beautiful pink sausages strung together, which a lady had dropped out of her bag. Horace pounced, and he had them in his mouth in an instant! The lady looked round and was horrified at what she saw.

'Stop thief!' she screamed, and again: 'Stop thief, stop! That dog has stolen my sausages! Help, help!' She went on like that for some time, screaming and waving her arms. Evidently she was very fond of sausages, too.

The only thing that Horace could do in the circumstances was to run. But the lady started to run, too, and she could run remarkably fast. What is more, some people who were standing around started to run as well, and they all chased Horace round the Market.

People had to jump out of the way to make room for them. But in doing so they knocked down the stalls, and they made a real mess of the piles of fruit and vegetables!

Horace managed to turn a corner, but there his way was blocked by the biggest, fiercest and ugliest dog he had ever seen in his life. This alarmed Horace so much that he opened his mouth – and dropped his sausages. The ugly dog snatched them up in an instant – and ran away.

'There he goes!' screamed the lady, who evidently mistook the ugly dog for Horace. 'After him!' So they chased the ugly dog this time, up the road and away. Horace, meanwhile, had had enough and ran back to Gumdrop. He felt quite tired and hungry after his adventure. If only he hadn't lost those sausages!

Just then Mr Oldcastle returned, quite
unaware of what had happened. He
patted Horace on the head.

'So you waited for me in Gumdrop
all this time!' he said. 'You are a very
good boy. Look – I've got something
for you.' And he gave Horace his
reward. A pair of lovely sausages!